peg + cat

NO LONGER PROP
Seattle Public L

10690171

THE SLEEPOVER

NewHolly Library

JAN 19 2019

JENNIFER OXLEY
+ BILLY ARONSON

CANDLEWICK
ENTERTAINMENT

Peg and Cat were in their pajamas
and were super-excited.
"Tonight we're having a sleepover--WITH PIRATES!"
said Peg.

Four Pirates in pajamas were jumping
up and down on Peg's bed.

"Awk! Am I not here?"
asked the parrot.

"Sorry," said Peg.
"We're having a
sleepover with Pirates
AND THE PARROT!"

The Pirates jumped down from the bed and
started drawing and playing board games.
Captain and Buckler scribbled wildly
as Peg used her favorite crayon,
Little Bluey, to draw rectangles.

3 + 1 = 4

Matey and Grey Beard played a board game with
Cat, who just kept spinning the arrow.
"I really like spinning," said Cat.

Next, the Pirates decided to have a . . .

4 + 1 = 5

PILLOW FIGHT!

6 + 1 = 7

"Okay, Pirates," said Peg. "It's bedtime.
We can have one last activity--if you
can all agree on something."

Two Pirates wanted a story; the other two didn't.
One Pirate wanted to listen to tunes;
the other three didn't.

7 + 1 = 8

Then the parrot suggested
something nobody
didn't want: TV!
They sat on the couch
and watched a music
video of the Pig dancing
on the Pirates' island.

Seeing their home, the Pirates felt homesick.
"WAAAAA!" they cried. "I WANTS ME MOMMY!"

"If we can't get the
Pirates to stop crying and
go to sleep, this will be the
worst sleepover ever,"
said Peg.
"We have A REALLY BIG PROBLEM!"

Peg and Cat put out sleeping bags, pillows,
and blankets to make the Pirates snug and cozy.
"We've got four sets of comfy sleeping stuff
for four Pirates," said Peg.

"Do I not matter?"
asked the parrot.

9+1=10

"Sorry," said Peg.
"Cat will add one more of each comfy thing
so there's enough for all five of you!"

"Four sleeping bags plus
one sleeping sock makes five
comfy things to sleep in,"
said Peg.

"Four pillows plus
one bean bag makes
five soft things
for your heads."

"Four blankets plus
one hankie makes
five soft things
for snuggling."

10+1=11

Cozy and comfy, the guests fell right to sleep.
The sleeping Pirates cuddled closer . . .
and closer . . . and closer,

until --

"AWK!"
screeched the parrot.
"A PIRATE RUBBED
HIS WHISKERS ON ME!"

12+1=13

"I'm awake again,"
said Captain.

"I'm more awake
than before,"
said Buckler.

"I'm the most
awake ever!"
said Matey.

Peg noticed Cat playing
with toy animals.

"That's it,
you genius sheep-holding Cat!"
said Peg.
"Counting sheep helps you
get to sleep!"

13+1=14

Peg only had three toy sheep.
"The Pirates will need to count a lot more
than three of something to get to sleep,"
Peg said.

But she only had six monkeys

and a giraffe and a half.
So Peg made a call.

From the phone came a loud "CHEEP!"
"Are chickens coming here?" asked Captain.

"Yes! You're going to get to sleep
by counting twenty of them,"
Peg replied.
"But we can only count to ten,"
said Buckler.

15+1=16

Cat pointed to number cards as Peg explained,
"After ten comes eleven and twelve.
Then come the teens: thirteen, fourteen, fifteen,
sixteen, seventeen, eighteen, nineteen.
Then comes a two with a zero after it--
that's twenty!"

16 + 1 = 17

The chickens were at the window.
"Come in and be counted, chickens!" said Peg.

17 + 1 = 18

18+1=19

The Pirates and the parrot got comfy
in their sleeping bags and sleeping sock.
As the chickens passed by one at a time,
the Pirates and the parrot counted,

"One, two, three, four, five, six, seven, eight, nine, ten."

19+1=20

As they counted past ten, they got sleepy.

"Eleven,

twelve,

thirteen,

fourteen,

fifteen."

20+1=21

For the rest of the teens,
they could barely keep their eyes open.

"Sixteen,

seventeen,

eighteen,

nineteen."

"Twenty!" whispered
the littlest chicken.

21 + 1 = 22

The Pirates and the parrot were fast asleep!
PROBLEM SOLVED!

22+1=23

This book is based on the TV series *Peg + Cat*.
Peg + Cat is produced by The Fred Rogers Company.
Created by Jennifer Oxley and Billy Aronson.
The Sleepover is based on a television script by Billy Aronson
and background art by Amy De Lay. Art assets assembled by Sarika Matthew.
The PBS KIDS logo is a registered mark of the
Public Broadcasting Service and is used with permission.

pbskids.org/peg

Copyright © 2018 Feline Features, LLC

All rights reserved. No part of this book may be reproduced, transmitted,
or stored in an information retrieval system in any form or by any means,
graphic, electronic, or mechanical, including photocopying, taping,
and recording, without prior written permission from the publisher.

First edition 2018

Library of Congress Catalog Card Number pending
ISBN 978-1-5362-0345-5

18 19 20 21 22 23 APS 10 9 8 7 6 5 4 3 2 1

Printed in Humen, Dongguan, China

This book was typeset in OPTITypewriter.
The illustrations were created digitally.

Candlewick Entertainment
an imprint of Candlewick Press
99 Dover Street
Somerville, Massachusetts 02144

visit us at www.candlewick.com